The

DAILY

COMET

BOY SAVES EARTH FROM GIANT OCTOPUS!

The DAILY COMET

WRITTEN BY FRANK ASCH

ILLUSTRATED BY DEVIN ASCH

KIDS CAN PRESS

Kids Can Press acknowledges the financial support of the
Government of Ontario, through the Ontario Media
Development Corporation's Ontario Book Initiative.

Published in Canada by
Kids Can Press Ltd.
29 Birch Avenue
Toronto, ON M4V 1E2

Published in the U.S. by
Kids Can Press Ltd.
2250 Military Road
Tonawanda, NY 14150

www.kidscanpress.com

Kids Can Press is a *corus*™ Entertainment company

The artwork in this book was rendered in Adobe Photoshop
and Corel Painter.
The text is set in ITC Cheltenham and Franklin Gothic.

Edited by Tara Walker
Designed by Karen Powers

This book is smyth sewn casebound.
Manufactured in Shenzhen, Guang Dong, P.R. China,
in 3/2010 by Printplus Limited

CM 10 0 9 8 7 6 5 4 3 2 1

Library and Archives Canada Cataloguing in Publication

Asch, Frank
The Daily comet : boy saves Earth from giant octopus! /
written by Frank Asch ; illustrated by Devin Asch.

ISBN 978-1-55453-281-0

I. Asch, Devin II. Title.

PZ7.A778Da 2010   j813'.54   C2009-906864-8

TO ARIAH AND EVELYN — F.A. & D.A.

HAYWARD HAD SEEN THE HUGE SKYSCRAPER WHERE HIS FATHER WORKED.

He had even ridden in the elevator to his office. But he had never sat at his dad's desk or met his boss before.

"What's that kid doing in the newsroom?" snapped the editor in chief. "If he wants a job, send him down to Personnel."

"Ah … Chief, this isn't just some kid looking for a job," said Roger Palmer, lead reporter for the *Daily Comet*. "This is my son, Hayward."

"Oh, yeah … *now* I remember!" Roger's boss shook Hayward's hand. "It's 'Go to Work with a Parent Day' for you, is it? Well … welcome aboard, Son!"

"Pleased to meet you," replied Hayward politely. But, in fact, he was *not* pleased to meet his dad's boss. As far as Hayward was concerned, the *Daily Comet* was a big fake and so was everyone who worked there.

"WHAT'S THE SCOOP TODAY, CHIEF?" ASKED ROGER.

"You want me to work on a follow-up to the flying spaghetti monster story?"

"Not today," said the chief. "There's a hot item just breaking at the Museum of Natural History. One of the dinosaur eggs cracked and is about to hatch! Have final copy on my desk by three o'clock."

Hayward rolled his eyes so far back in his head he could almost see his brain.

"I'll just read a book while you work, Dad," he said.

"Sorry, Son," replied his father. "We're going to have to go out and do some interviewing for this one."

Interviewing? thought Hayward. *Who is Dad trying to kid? Everyone knows all the stories in the* Daily Comet *are made-up rubbish.*

"Oh, yeah," said the chief as he was about to return to his office. "Take Alfonzo with you. We're going to want some pictures."

THE MUSEUM OF NATURAL HISTORY WAS ACTUALLY ONE OF HAYWARD'S FAVORITE PLACES.

Hayward liked facts. Plain, simple, scientific facts. As they left the *Daily Comet* office and took the subway to the museum, he looked forward to seeing the latest exhibits.

But there was no time for browsing. Upon arrival they went straight to the dinosaur room where a crowd of expectant museum-goers had already gathered.

While Roger interviewed the curator, Alfonzo photographed the cracked egg.

"I wouldn't bother doing that," said Hayward. "That egg is undoubtedly a fake."

"Sure looks down-home real to me," replied Alfonzo.

"If this isn't a publicity stunt, then I'm sure my dad set up this whole preposterous situation for my benefit," said Hayward with a sigh.

"Now why would he do somethin' like that?" asked Alfonzo.

"To convince me that the other weird stories he writes are real. But it's not going to work. I'm no dummy. I know million-year-old dinosaur eggs can't hatch. It's impossible."

Just then the dinosaur egg split wide open …

"HOLY CATFISH! A BRAND NEW BABY DINOSAUR!" EXCLAIMED ALFONZO, SNAPPING PICTURES.

"You still think that egg is a fake?"

"Are you kidding me?" said Hayward. "That's no baby dinosaur. It's a full-grown lizard and whoever stuck it in that phony egg is perpetrating a hoax."

Roger's phone rang. It was the chief.

"Listen up, Roger," he barked. "Drop the dinosaur story and hop a cab over to Times Square ASAP. A ten-foot-tall chicken was just spotted crossing Forty-second and Broadway."

"We're on the way, Chief!" said Roger.

"Oh, and Roger," added the chief, "don't forget to play up the why-did-the-chicken-cross-the-road angle."

"Sure thing," said Hayward's father.

OUTSIDE THE MUSEUM, ROGER HAILED THE FIRST CAB HE SAW.

"Dig it!" cried Alfonzo as the cab pulled up to the curb. "It's our old friend, Sam."

"Good to see you two again," said the huge, hairy man behind the steering wheel.

"Same here," said Hayward's father, opening the cab door. "Take us to Times Square and step on it!"

"HOWZIT GOING, MAN?" ASKED ALFONZO

as the big yellow cab pulled out into traffic.

"Terrific," said Sam. "After you two did that feature article about me in the *Daily Comet*, I was invited to enroll in the Bigfoot Relocation Program. And they got me this job driving a cab. The hours are long and you meet some really weird characters in the wee hours of the morning, but the money is great! With any luck, this time next winter I'll have enough saved up to visit my folks in Siberia."

Siberia? My eye, thought Hayward. *I bet anything this Bigfoot phony comes from Brooklyn.*

"How much do we owe you?" asked Roger when they reached Times Square.

"You guys always ride for free in my cab," said Sam, handing Hayward's father his card. "Whenever you need a lift, just dial my number and I'll be there faster than an avalanche!"

"I'M FLATTERED THAT YOU WENT TO ALL THAT TROUBLE TO IMPRESS ME,"

said Hayward as Sam's cab pulled away from the curb. "But I'm not a little kid anymore. I know that was just some guy in a hairy costume. Bigfoot is a myth. He doesn't exist!"

"Have it your way," said his father.

"Dig it!" Alfonzo pointed to a crowd of people gathered around a smashed-up hot dog stand.

Roger whipped out his notebook and pencil. "Anyone mind telling me what happened here?"

I know what happened here, thought Hayward. *My dad just staged another hoax. That's what happened.*

"A giant chicken attacked my stand," complained the hot dog vendor. "Ate all my hot dogs, drank all my lemonade and then ran down into the subway! Meanest ten-foot chicken I ever saw!"

Alfonzo popped off a few quick shots of the wreckage. "We gonna follow it, boss?"

"You bet," said Roger. "But this chicken sounds dangerous." He handed Hayward a ten dollar bill. "It's almost noon. Buy yourself some lunch and wait for us right here!"

"Sure, Dad," said Hayward.

"Hey, man, if you spot any fried peanut butter sandwiches, grab me one," said Alfonzo.

AS HAYWARD BOUGHT HIMSELF A SLICE OF PIZZA, HE NOTICED A MAN

wearing a porkpie hat and a bow tie setting up a small table nearby.

"Step right up and sample the most amazing beverage ever!" announced the man loudly. "And it costs only pennies!"

Right, thought Hayward, but having nothing better to do, he wandered over to see what the man was selling.

"We have here an ordinary glass." The man put a drinking glass on his table. "Now, would anyone like to lend me the contents of their pockets? Anything metal will do."

Hayward pulled out his pocketknife and offered it to the man, who dropped it into the glass with a flourish.

A bystander offered her car keys. Another handed over his wristwatch. Pretty soon the glass was full.

"Thank you very much," said the man, taking a small brown bottle from his pocket. "Now I have here the world's most fantastic elixir ever created!"

"WHAT DOES IT DO?" ASKED THE WOMAN WHO HAD DONATED HER CAR KEYS.

"Excellent question!" said the man as he unscrewed the cap and carefully poured a few drops of green liquid into the glass. "It turns anything metal into a nutritious health drink."

The crowd gasped as the man lifted the glass to his lips and drank its contents.

"Ah!" he said, wiping green foam from his mouth. "And it tastes delicious, too!"

The crowd, of course, was irate.

"Hey, give me back my pocketknife!" demanded Hayward.

"What have you done with my car keys?!" cried the woman.

"Sorry, madam, I just drank your car keys," replied the man. "But don't worry. I'll give you a special discount on your first bottle of my fantastic elixir!"

"*Discount?!* Why you charlatan! You sleight-of-hand creep!" The woman rolled up her sleeves, grabbed the man by his collar and lifted him up in the air. As she did, the little brown bottle of elixir fell onto the sidewalk.

Hayward picked up the bottle. But before he could trade it back for his pocketknife, Alfonzo tapped him on the shoulder.

"CHECK OUT THESE PICS!"

said Alfonzo.

"Turns out this chicken wasn't so dangerous after all," Hayward's father explained. "In fact, she's a Latin scholar and a math whiz. But she does have some anger management problems due to her unusual size."

"*Sure*," said Hayward. "And the moon is made of green cheese."

"Actually, I once wrote a piece about that very subject," said Roger.

"I know, Dad," said Hayward with a sigh.

By then the police had come for the man selling his elixir, and everyone was pointing up to the sky.

"Look, it's a bird! It's a plane!" they cried. "No, it's a … FLYING CUP AND SAUCER!"

"IT'S HEADED TOWARD CENTRAL PARK,"

said Roger, calling Sam on his phone.

Minutes later, Sam dropped them off near the duck pond as the huge flying cup and saucer landed.

"I guess you think this is a stunt of some kind, too, don't you, Hayward?" asked his father.

"Absolutely," said Hayward. "It's probably a promotion for a new sci-fi movie. Everyone knows Hollywood movies have enormous budgets nowadays."

"Let's move closer," said Alfonzo. "I want a close-up of the aliens comin' out."

Slowly, from the depths of the teacup, an enormous metallic octopus emerged.

"ARE YOU ON THE UFO STORY?"

the chief barked over Roger's phone.

"Yeah, we're on it, boss," said Hayward's father. "Any chance this octopus could be friendly?"

"No way!" replied the chief. "According to the top-secret radio transmissions we intercepted, it intends to drain Earth's oceans and take all our water back to its own planet."

A glimmer of doubt flickered in Hayward's mind. *Could Dad really have planned all this?* he wondered.

Just then the octopus snatched a statue off its pedestal and hurled it into the pond.

Hayward craned his neck to catch a glimpse of who was creating this spectacle. But there were no movie directors, cameras or theatrical lights to be seen.

WITHOUT WARNING, THE OCTOPUS CURLED ITS MECHANICAL TENTACLES AROUND HAYWARD

and his father and slunk out of the park.

Hayward was finally beginning to think this wasn't a publicity stunt after all.

"Um … Dad," he confessed in a small, shaky voice, "this is really scaring me!"

"Sorry, Son," said Roger. "I guess you picked the wrong day to come visit me at work."

Suddenly Hayward remembered the little brown bottle.

"No, Dad," he declared as he reached into his pocket. "It's definitely the *right* day!"

HAYWARD QUICKLY UNCORKED THE BOTTLE

and poured its contents onto the giant octopus.

Instantly the creature's tentacles went limp and it was enshrouded in a cloud of smoke. When the smoke cleared, all that remained was an enormous puddle of nutritious green liquid.

"I don't know how you did that, Hayward," said Roger as he gave his son a hug "but you sure saved the day!"

It was at that moment that Alfonzo took the picture that appeared on the front page of the next issue of the *Daily Comet* with the caption:

BOY SAVES EARTH FROM GIANT OCTOPUS!

OF COURSE, WHEN HAYWARD BROUGHT THE ARTICLE INTO CLASS

to accompany his "Go to Work with a Parent Day" report, no one believed him.

"I didn't believe it at first either," said Hayward. "But it *really* did happen! Every word of this article is true."

"*Sure!*" said Ronald Winfrey. "How can you expect us to accept that when your father wrote it?"

"So what?" said Hayward. "If you don't believe the story, just look at the photograph!"

"Photographs can be faked," said Dorothy Lurch. "It's easy!"

"Believe what you want," said Hayward. "All I know is that my dad is the world's greatest reporter!"

"Yeah, well, I think he's a fake," said Larry Chompsky, and he blew a spitball at the article.

"That's enough!" cried Miss Monroe. "We're moving on to our next report. Let's see …" She consulted her list. "Next up is our new student who spent a day with her father, a taxicab driver in New York City."

Mary Geddy's Day

A Colonial Girl in Williamsburg

by KATE WATERS

photographed by RUSS KENDALL

IN ASSOCIATION WITH THE COLONIAL WILLIAMSBURG FOUNDATION

SCHOLASTIC PRESS ⮀ NEW YORK

For Mary Ellen, my mother and my friend
— K. W.

In memory of Jim Carson, my dad
— R. K.

Acknowledgments

Making a book is a team effort. We give heartfelt thanks to the marvelous cast — Emily Smith as Mary Geddy, Stewart Sensor as James Geddy III, Jeremiah Smith as William Geddy, Sarah Sensor as Elizabeth Geddy, Frances Burroughs as Mrs. Geddy (and den mother to us all), Terry Yemm as Mr. Geddy, Dakari Taylor-Watson as Christopher, Monica Spry as Nan, Valerie Perry as Grace, Caitlin Graft as Anne, Carolyn Randall as Hattie, and John Barrows as Mr. Pelham.

We also wish to acknowledge the parents of our young actors, who were with us at all times and helped in so many ways: Chuck and Sharon Smith, Anita Sensor and Roy Heffley, and Robert Watson.

And we thank everyone from Colonial Williamsburg — those in front of the camera and those behind the scenes — for helping us bring Mary Geddy's day to life. "Huzzah" to you all.

We thank Suzanne Coffman, copilot extraordinaire; Amy Edmondson, second in command; Thérèse Landry, photographer's assistant; Marijka Kostiw, designer; and Dianne Hess, our editor, for their commitment and support.

The recipe on page 38 is from *Recipes from the Raleigh Tavern Bake Shop*, published by The Colonial Williamsburg Foundation.

Library of Congress Cataloging-in-Publication Data

Waters, Kate. Mary Geddy's day: a colonial girl in Williamsburg / by Kate Waters; photographs by Russ Kendall. p. cm.

ISBN 0-590-92925-9

1. Williamsburg (Va.)—History—Revolution, 1775–1783—Juvenile fiction. [1. Williamsburg (Va.)—History—Revolution, 1775–1783—Fiction. 2. United States—History—Revolution, 1775–1783—Fiction.] I. Kendall, Russ, ill. II. Title. PZ7.W26434Mar 1999 [Fic]—dc21 98-46274   CIP AC
10 9 8 7 6 5 4 3 2 1   9/9 0/0 01 02 03 04

Printed in Hong Kong • 38 • First edition, September 1999

The display type was set in A Caslon Expert Swash Semibold Italic. • The text type was set in Stempel Schneidler. • Book design by Marijka Kostiw

Prologue

In 1776, 169 years after the first English settlers came to Jamestown, there were thirteen colonies along the Atlantic Ocean. They were ruled by the king of England, George III. People in the colonies had to obey the laws of England. Each colony also elected its own legislature, which made laws for the colony and taxed the people who lived there.

After the Seven Years' War ended in 1763, England needed money. The British government decided to tax the colonies. The colonists felt these taxes were wrong. They argued that only the colonial legislatures should tax them.

"No taxation without representation," the colonists said.

Most of the colonists felt they should remain loyal to their king. But as more and more taxes were established, people began to believe that the British government would never respect the colonists' rights. More and more people wanted to set up an independent country.

On May 15, 1776, in Williamsburg, Virginia, a group of patriot leaders voted to declare Virginia free from Great Britain. They also voted to ask the other colonies to do the same. This action set in motion the events that eventually freed all thirteen colonies from British rule. These colonies were to become the United States of America.

Let us find out what it might have been like at Mary Geddy's house on that day.

How do you do? I am Mary Geddy of Williamsburg in the colony of Virginia. My papa is a silversmith. We are nine persons in our household: Papa and Mama, my brother James, who is upwards of twelve years, myself, just ten years, my brother William, who is eight years, and my sister, Elizabeth, who is six years. Grace, her son, Christopher, and Nan are our slaves.

This is an important day in my town. Visitors from all parts crowd the streets and taverns. Today the delegates to the Fifth Virginia Convention will either vote to remain a colony of Great Britain — or they will vote for independence.

I am both excited and frightened, since my life will surely change. I do not often listen to talk of politics, but today's events may mean war. And they may also mean I will be parted from my best friend.

Very early, when I wake up, I hear people abroad.

I wake my sister, Elizabeth, wash my face and hands, change my cap, and get dressed.

Nan comes in to lace my stays. They help me to stand up straight.

1. Waking up

5. Shoes

6. Stays

7. Petticoat and pocket

2. Washing

3. Shift and stockings

4. Garters

8. Gown

I help Elizabeth tie her ribbon.

Christopher carries out the chamber pot while I straighten the room.

Elizabeth and I tiptoe downstairs. Mama likes us to be still in the morning.

Mama gives me coins and sends me to get fresh eggs at the market. I tuck the coins into my pocket, put on my kerchief and hat, and close the door quietly.

Our house is in the middle of town, where Duke of Gloucester Street and Palace Street meet. Papa sells his silver work in the shop next to our house. Two of my uncles have a foundry in the backyard. There they repair all sorts of metal goods and make splendid new ones, too.

See how busy the town is today! Even at this early hour, there is excitement in the air.

At the market, I find Grace's friend Hattie and give her coins for the eggs.

My best friend, Anne, and I stop to talk. Anne's papa is loyal to the king. If the vote today is for independence, her family will return to England. My papa is a patriot. He will be pleased to be free from British rule. Our family will stay in Virginia. Even though our papas are on different sides, Anne and I have been best friends since we were small. My insides curl when I think of saying good-bye to my friend. Freedom will not feel as good to me if Anne must leave.

On the way home I pass some delegates who are arguing loudly. They are talking about the vote. That is all the talk I have heard for many days!

Back at home, I give Grace the eggs and go in to
breakfast. Nan pours coffee for Mama and Papa, and
cider for us children. The hot hoecakes and apple butter
taste good. The early morning air has made me hungry.

"There are so many people abroad, Mama," I tell her.
"May we walk about after breakfast?"

"I want you to keep to the house, Mary," she says.
"There is no telling how people will behave. It may be a
while before we know any news."

James is fortunate. He goes to work in the shop with
Papa. He will hear all of the news there!

13

William and I help put the room at rest before our lessons. I take my sewing basket to the window so I can watch the street. I am stitching a sampler. When I am finished with my letters, I will stitch the numbers. At least I am not to do mending today. That is a task I dislike.

14

Elizabeth is just learning her letters. She would rather ask for help than think the alphabet through herself.

William is not worth a button. He pretends to be a fifer playing a liberty song.

"Go to the shop, William," says Mama. "Perhaps you can help polish the silver." How fortunate to be a boy and not be kept away from the excitement.

It is hard to sit still. After a time, Mama takes me to the kitchen. She has promised to teach me to make a pie.

I pour water on the dried apples to make them plump. Then I grind the spices.

Next we flour the board to roll the crust.

"Not too fat and not too thin," Mama says. That is easier said than done!

After I lay the crust in the pan, Mama shows me how to cut the edges. I put in half the apples and sprinkle sugar and spices and lemon peel on top.

After the pie is filled with the rest of the apples and spices, I put on the top crust. The pie is plump and high when it is finished.

"Look, Grace. My first pie!"

"I'll bake it for your dinner," she says.

I think Grace is proud of me. I have never been much use in the kitchen before!

I collect Elizabeth, and we go outside to help Nan in the garden. I pick lettuce and weed a little.

We check the cherries to see if they are ripe yet.

18

I see Anne passing by, and I call
her to the fence.
"Can you visit awhile?" I ask.

We sit close together.

"I do not want to return to England," she says. "I won't know anyone!"

"I promise I'll write to you," I answer.

"Can we post letters during a war?" Anne asks.

Talk of war makes us both quiet. We tie the lavender she has picked into bundles to dry. We will make sweet bags for linen from it — if Anne is still here.

When Anne goes home, Elizabeth calls to me from the swing. I can tell that she is frightened.

"I heard Anne say 'war,' Mary. Will we still have a war?" she asks.

"The delegates are not voting for war," I tell her. "They are voting for or against independence."

I don't want Elizabeth to know that I am as frightened as she is. I try to make her smile by pushing her high on the swing.

"Dinner will be ready soon," Mama calls from the back door. "Call your papa and your brothers, Mary, and you and Elizabeth come clean to the table."

I go to the shop to call Papa and James and William.
There is a crowd there. Most are talking, not buying.

"Is there any news, Papa?" I ask.

"Not yet, Mary," he answers. "You must be patient.
Perhaps the soldiers will fire their guns when the vote
is counted."

Papa says a prayer before dinner.

"God bless us in what we are to receive."

There is an abundance of food — too much for
my nervous appetite. There is roast chicken, fried
oysters, peas, potatoes, salad, sweet potato fritters,
bread, and my apple pie. There is so much talk about
independence, no one remembers that this is my
first pie.

When dinner is over, we say, "God make us thankful for His mercies." I don't know how thankful I can be if I must part from Anne.

After dinner, Papa and James go back to the shop. Since Elizabeth still looks pale and has eaten little, Mama sends William and me to the store to buy a treat to comfort her. I choose the sugar candy she likes. She can make it last a long time.

Back home, Mr. Pelham, the music teacher, has arrived. He is teaching me to play the spinet pleasingly. My fingers are almost worn down when it is time to stop.

Suddenly there is a great commotion outside on the street. We run upstairs to the balcony.

BOOM! BOOM! BOOM! I can hear round after round of gunfire. "Independence!" is shouted up and down the street. William points to the Capitol. I can see the gun smoke from here! I must go, I think. For once I must see what is happening.

We wait for Papa to close the shop. Finally he comes. "Let us go down to the Capitol at once," he says.

Elizabeth is too frightened to go. Papa tells her to stay in the house with Nan and play with Christopher. I know that Christopher is disappointed. I wish he could come, too.

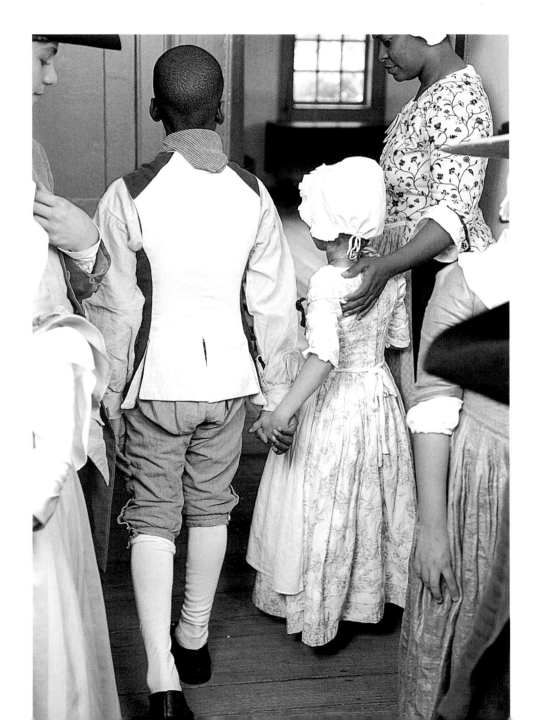

As we walk down the street to the Capitol, I see Anne looking over her gate.

"Come with us," I call.

"My papa won't allow me," she says. "He is not pleased with the vote. He has asked for our trunks. We are planning to leave."

Suddenly independence does not seem so exciting to me. Can it be a good decision that separates two friends?

When we reach the Capitol, the British flag
is being lowered down the flagpole.

In a moment the continental flag, the flag
of George Washington's army, is raised.
Virginia has decided. Our thirteen colonies
should be an independent country!

The gunshots are loud and there are shouts of
"Huzzah! Huzzah! Huzzah!" again and again.

When it gets late, we must return home. Papa and Mama are having guests for supper. On the way, we see a man taking down the sign at the King's Arms Tavern. The colonies shall no longer have a king!

At home, Elizabeth and I help Mama get ready for supper. Mama's face is pink with excitement. We help her place her breast knot.

"Your papa will take care of us all, my girls," Mama says. "You must not worry overmuch."

But I wonder if Papa knows how much I will miss Anne. I wonder if he can keep us safe in a big war.

I have not much of a hunger for supper, but my pie still tastes good. William and Elizabeth say that it is delicious!

After supper, I read *Aesop's Fables* to Elizabeth and William.

Nan comes to put us to bed. On the way, we greet Papa's guests in the parlor. I make my best courtesy and kiss Mama good night.

Upstairs, I steal out to the balcony.
The cressets burn in the dark street.
The town seems to be crazy
with delight.

I get ready for bed and tuck Elizabeth in. When she is still, I go to the window. I wonder how my life will change because of this day. Will Papa go to war? Will we be able to stay in this town, or will there be fighting here? Will I still have music lessons? Will Anne truly move away — all the way to England? Will we still be friends when we are so far apart?

I climb into our bed and know I must wait for answers. Papa seems so certain that independence will be best for this country. We will see what this day means for us all.

Good night to you.

Treasure your friends.

Sleep well always.

Notes About the Book

Williamsburg in Colonial Times

Virginia was the first permanent colony established by England in North America. In 1607, a group of settlers arrived in Virginia. They made their way up the James River to a place they named Jamestown. Jamestown was the capital of the colony until 1699, when Williamsburg was founded. Williamsburg was Virginia's capital until 1780.

In 1776, when this story takes place, Virginia was the largest of the thirteen original colonies. The other colonies were Georgia, South Carolina, North Carolina, Maryland, Pennsylvania, Delaware, Rhode Island, New Jersey, New York, Connecticut, Massachusetts, and New Hampshire.

Williamsburg was a busy, thriving town surrounded by plantations. The College of William and Mary, Bruton Parish Church, and the Capitol building were important landmarks. Many artisans and tradespeople lived and worked in town. You could have a new wig, a hat, a saddle, a pair of shoes, or a silver candlestick made there. The many taverns in Williamsburg offered food and lodging to the visitors who came to town to conduct business or to serve in the legislature.

Four times a year, in April, June, October, and December, Publick Times were held in Williamsburg. During Publick Times, the high courts were in session. The town's population, about 1,500 in the 1770s, made room for several hundred more people during these periods.

If the legislature was in session, burgesses from all around the colony met in Williamsburg to enact laws and respond to communications from England. Burgesses were elected representatives who served in the House of Burgesses, the lower house of the Virginia legislature. The governor and his Council of twelve prominent Virginians had to approve the legislation, which was then forwarded to England for approval by the king and his ministers.

Publick Times were also times for balls, entertaining, and going to the theater. They were the main social seasons in Williamsburg.

The Prelude to Independence

During the 158 years after the founding of Jamestown, Virginia went from a struggling outpost to a thriving colony. Virginians became experienced at running their colony. But they did not think of independence. People in the other colonies felt the same way.

However, in 1765, England imposed a new tax, called the Stamp Act, on the colonies. The citizens were outraged. Britain had taxed the Americans even though the colonies had no members in the British legislature to represent them.

Even though the Stamp Act was repealed, Britain imposed new laws during the following years. One law, the Tea Act, gave an English company, the East India Company, exclusive rights to sell tea in the colonies. This law was unfair to the colonial merchants who sold tea. On December 16, 1773, a group of men boarded a ship in Boston Harbor and tossed hundreds of chests of tea overboard. In May 1774, Virginians learned that the port of Boston would be closed on June 1 in retaliation for the Boston Tea Party. Virginia's leaders proposed a boycott of English goods. Many Virginians, including the Geddy family, stopped drinking tea and buying items from England.

In Virginia and the other colonies, the desire for independence began to grow. In April 1775, violence almost broke out in Williamsburg when the governor ordered British marines to take away the colony's gunpowder. Then news reached Williamsburg of the battles at Lexington and Concord in Massachusetts. In June, Virginia's governor fled the capital. Some Virginians decided to move their families to England. It was common for friends like Mary and Anne to have to part.

In May 1776, delegates gathered in Williamsburg. While they were meeting, the Continental Congress was meeting in Philadelphia. On May 15, the day on which this story takes place, the delegates voted to adopt the Resolution for Independence. Three weeks later, Virginian Richard Henry Lee stood before the Continental Congress and proposed that the "United Colonies" break away from Great Britain. On July 4, the representatives accepted the Declaration of Independence. The United States of America was born.

British and American forces fought until October 19, 1781, when British General Cornwallis surrendered his forces to George Washington at Yorktown, Virginia, near Williamsburg. The Revolution ended officially on September 3, 1783, when the United States and England signed the Treaty of Paris.

Slavery in the Virginia Colony

The first blacks had arrived in Virginia by 1619. During the first half of the 1600s, the few people of African descent in the colony were not slaves. But by mid-century, white Virginians had passed slave laws. After that, people captured in Africa and sold in Virginia were used by plantation owners, merchants, and tradespeople to do hard labor, to cook, to keep house, to take care of white children, and to carry goods around town. Slaves were considered the property of their masters for life. They had few rights.

Native Americans in Colonial Virginia

By 1776, the native peoples that lived in Virginia all either lived on reservations or had moved to the frontier. Much of Virginia had once been the Powhatan Empire. More than thirty tribes — the Pamunkies, Chickahominys, and Mattaponis among them — had lived there.

Native American delegations did visit Williamsburg to pay tribute to the governor or to petition the colonial government. Others came to town to trade. And people of Native American ancestry probably lived in the area, but had changed their names or married white or free black people.

The Geddy Family

James Geddy, Jr., and his family were considered "of the middling sort." That means they were not as wealthy as large plantation owners or well-to-do merchants. And they were not poor people — of the "lower sort" — who worked for other people or on small farms. The Geddys were prominent tradesmen. Tradesmen worked with their hands as silversmiths, blacksmiths, founders, tailors, or builders. The Geddys lived very comfortably and worked to give their children educational opportunities and a secure place in life.

James's family probably came to North America from Scotland. The first mention of the name "Geddy" appears in Williamsburg records from 1733.

Mary and her family moved away from Williamsburg in 1778. In 1789, when she was twenty-three, Mary married William Prentis, a printer. She and her husband lived in Petersburg, Virginia, on property her father gave her.

Girlhood in Eighteenth-Century Williamsburg

The main responsibility of young girls in the eighteenth century was to learn "the arts and mysteries of housewifery." They learned about the running of a house, about cooking, and about shopping so that they could manage their households when they married.

Girls also learned to play musical instruments, to dance, to sew, to read aloud, and to pay attention to the fashions of the day. Girls like Mary Geddy did not do very hard chores, but their days were busy.

Sewing samplers was a way for young girls to practice stitches. Samplers had the alphabet, numbers, sometimes a religious verse, a picture, and the girl's name and the date when she finished the sampler. Some people in the eighteenth century used an alphabet that had only twenty-four letters. They did not use "J" or "U." Instead, people used "I" and "V," especially on samplers and tombstones.

Children in Mary Geddy's kind of family read a great deal. Popular books of the time included fables, histories, cookbooks, books of manners, and religious books.

Making Sweet Bags for Linen from Lavender

Lavender has been used for many, many years to make rooms and drawers smell fresh. Pick or buy lavender when the flowers are bright purple. Tie several stalks together and hang them to dry upside down in a dim place. After the flowers are dry, spread a cloth under the lavender and gently shake the stalks. The dried flowers will fall off.

Take a rectangular piece of pretty cloth and fold it in half. Sew together two sides of the cloth to make a pouch. Fill it with the dried flowers. Then sew up the open side. Your lavender "sweet bag for linen," which today we call a "sachet," will be fragrant for a long time.

Apple Pie Recipe

This is an authentic recipe from Colonial Williamsburg.

PASTRY

3 cups all-purpose flour

1 teaspoon salt

*1 cup shortening
   (up to 1/4 of which may be butter)*

1 egg, lightly beaten

1/2 cup very cold water

Combine the flour and salt. Add the shortening and cut the mixture with a knife or a pastry blender until it is mealy. Add the beaten egg and 1/4 cup of the water. Gradually add the remaining water, if necessary, to make a soft pastry. Chill well. On a floured surface, roll out two round crusts about 1/8 inch thick.

APPLE FILLING

7 to 8 tart apples, peeled and sliced

*1 tablespoon lemon juice
    (instead of the lemon peel Mary uses)*

3/4 to 1 cup sugar

2 tablespoons flour

*1/2 teaspoon cinnamon (Mary didn't use cinnamon
    because it came from Ceylon and was very expensive,
    but the pie tastes better with it.)*

1/4 teaspoon nutmeg

1/4 teaspoon ground cloves

1/8 teaspoon mace

1 to 2 tablespoons butter

Sprinkle the apple slices with lemon juice. Combine the sugar, flour, cinnamon, nutmeg, cloves, and mace. Add the apple slices and mix gently until they are well coated. Fill the pastry-lined pie plate with the apple mixture. Dot with the butter. Add the top crust. Press the edges together firmly and slash vents in the center of the crust. Dust with sugar for sparkle if desired. Bake in a preheated 400° F oven for 50 to 60 minutes or until the apples are done and the crust is golden brown.

Who Is Emily Smith?

Emily Smith, who plays Mary Geddy in this book, was nine years old and in third grade when the photographs for this book were taken. She has always been interested in Colonial Williamsburg because her father works there. Since the photo shoot, Emily has become a Junior Interpreter at the Geddy House. She says, "Thanks to this book, I have a knowledge of the Geddy family and how they lived. As an interpreter I dress in costume and talk to our visitors about the daily life of a colonial child. I interpret eighteenth-century games, catechism lessons, and playing cricket. My favorite part of being an interpreter is talking with visitors. My least favorite part is the process of dressing, because we have so many layers of clothing to put on."

When not enjoying eighteenth-century life, Emily likes to read, swim, and play the recorder and violin.

About Colonial Williamsburg

Colonial Williamsburg is the largest and oldest living history museum in the world. The museum's Historic Area has been restored to look the way it did in the 1770s, when Williamsburg was the capital of Britain's Virginia colony. Here Patrick Henry, Thomas Jefferson, George Washington, and other patriots rallied Virginians to the Revolutionary cause and helped lead the thirteen colonies to independence. Today, costumed interpreters bring to life the men, women, and children — white and black, free and enslaved, rich and poor — who lived and worked in eighteenth-century Williamsburg. Horse-drawn wagons and carriages roll down the streets. Patient oxen, long-wooled sheep, and colorful poultry inhabit pastures and pens, completing the picture of the town as it was more than two hundred years ago. A visit to Colonial Williamsburg is a step back in time to the era of the American Revolution.

Glossary